SCOOBY-DOO!™
BAKE-OFF MAYHEM

Written by Lee Howard
Illustrated by Alcadia SNC

ABDOPUBLISHING.COM

Reinforced library bound edition published in 2016 by Spotlight, a division of ABDO
PO Box 398166, Minneapolis, Minnesota 55439. Spotlight produces high-quality
reinforced library bound editions for schools and libraries. Published by agreement
with Warner Bros. Entertainment Inc.

Printed in the United States of America, North Mankato, Minnesota.
092015
012016

THIS BOOK CONTAINS
RECYCLED MATERIALS

CATALOGING-IN-PUBLICATION DATA

Howard, Lee.
 Scooby-Doo in bake-off mayhem / Lee Howard.
  p. cm. (Scooby-Doo leveled readers)
 Summary: Someone is ruining all the pies at the Country Fair Bake-Off. Can Scooby-Doo solve
 the mystery and find sweet success?
 1. Scooby-Doo (Fictitious character)--Juvenile fiction. 2. Dogs--Juvenile fiction. 3. Mystery and
 detective stories--Juvenile fiction. 4. Adventure and adventures--Juvenile fiction.
 [Fic]--dc23
         2015156079

 978-1-61479-418-9   (Reinforced Library Bound Edition)

Spotlight
A Division of ABDO
abdopublishing.com

It was a perfect day for Scooby-Doo and the gang to visit the country fair.

"Hey, Scoob! Do you smell what I smell?" asked Shaggy.

"Rummy!" said Scooby.

"Look!" said Shaggy. "Like, there's a bake-off contest!"
Elmer Jones sat at the judge's table.

"I may have to cancel the contest," he said sadly.
"Why?" Fred asked.
"Someone is spoiling all the desserts," said Elmer.

"I know. Shaggy and Scooby can enter the contest and we can catch the culprit," said Fred.

"Great!" said Elmer.

"This is my family recipe for blackberry pie," said Shaggy.
The gang takes a taste.
"Yummy!" they cry.

The gang met the Dumpling Sisters. "Welcome to the bake-off!" said Mary-Lou and Tiffany. "We've won three years in a row."

"Ruh?" Scooby said. He saw that they were twins.

"We are baking against each other this year," said Tiffany.

Pierre, a French pastry chef, was at the next station.
"Pardon, you're in my way!" he said.

Dwayne, a short-order cook, was next to Pierre.

"You're crowding me, guys!" said Dwayne.

The judge tasted the desserts.
He made a sour face.
"Yuck!" said Elmer. "These desserts all taste sour!"

"But Shaggy's cake was delicious!" Velma said.
"Hmmm," said Daphne. "This is very strange."
"You all have to start over!" said Elmer.

"We better get cracking, Scoob!" said Shaggy.
"Rup!" said Scooby.

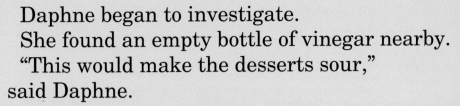

Daphne began to investigate.
She found an empty bottle of vinegar nearby.
"This would make the desserts sour,"
said Daphne.

15

Elmer tasted the new batch of desserts.
He smiled when he tasted Shaggy's.
"Delicious," said Elmer.

Elmer announced the finalists. Everyone but Dwayne was chosen.

Dwayne was angry.

"I'll show you!" he threatened.

It was time for the contest.
Scooby took a taste.

He pointed to the cake.
"What's wrong, Scoob?" asked Shaggy.
Daphne tasted it. "Sour again."

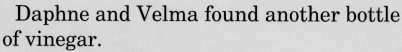

Daphne and Velma found another bottle of vinegar.
It was by Pierre's station.
"That's not mine," he said.

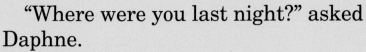

"Where were you last night?" asked Daphne.

"I was at my restaurant," said Pierre. "Ask my boss."

"What's that?" asked Fred.
He pointed to a hat on the ground.
It was next to Mary-Lou's station.
Daphne picked it up. "It's Dwayne's hat!"

Mary-Lou tasted her cake. "It's ruined!"
"Did Dwayne do this?" asked Fred.
"I wonder..." said Daphne.

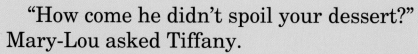

"How come he didn't spoil your dessert?" Mary-Lou asked Tiffany.

"My cake is too good to ruin," said Tiffany.

"Oh, yeah?" Mary-Lou picked up her cake and threw it at her sister.

Tiffany ducked. The cake hit Shaggy in the face!

"Right back at you!" cried Shaggy as he threw his dessert at Mary-Lou.

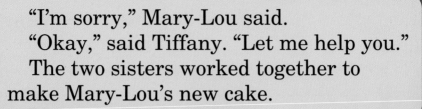

"I'm sorry," Mary-Lou said.
"Okay," said Tiffany. "Let me help you."
The two sisters worked together to make Mary-Lou's new cake.

Shaggy and Scooby baked another cake, too.
"Like, I hope this is the last time," said Shaggy.
"I'll help you guys," Tiffany said.

Tiffany dropped her whisk.
Daphne picked it up.
She tapped Tiffany on the shoulder.

"What?' Tiffany said.
She quickly put something in
her pocket.

Later, Elmer tasted all the desserts.
All were sour except for one.
"Only Tiffany's cake tastes good," Elmer
declared.

"That makes me the winner!" said Tiffany.
"Wait one second." Daphne stepped forward.
She reached into Tiffany's pocket and pulled
out a bottle of vinegar!
"I knew it was you all along!" cried Mary-Lou.

"Tiffany is out of the bake-off!" said Elmer. The other contestants baked one last time. "Shaggy and Scooby are the winners!" said Elmer.

"Scooby-Dooby-Doo!"